County Council

Libraries, books and more...........

Please return/renew this item by the last date shown.
Library items may also be renewed by phone on
030 33 33 1234 (24hours) or via our website

www.cumbria.gov.uk/libraries

Cumbria Libraries

CLIC

Interactive Catalogue

Ask for a CLIC password

You are Arthur, King of the Britons. Your magical sword Excalibur is a symbol of your power and authority over the land.

Since your reign began, you have gathered together many knights at your castle of Camelot, where you sit with them at the Round Table, ruling the land fairly and fighting against injustice.

However, there are still people in Britain who do not want you as their king. With the Knights of the Round Table, you have fought many successful battles against your enemies, but you know that there are still people plotting against you. You must always be on your guard.

Go to 1.

1

You are travelling back to Camelot with
Sir Lancelot from the northern lands, where
you have defeated the latest rebellion against
you. It was a hard campaign and the other
Knights of the Round Table have stayed in the
north to keep the peace, but you have decided
that you must return to your castle.

You are riding along a riverbank, when, in the
blink of an eye, a white blanket of fog engulfs
you. You can see nothing through the thick,
white cloud.

"This is strange," you say to Lancelot.
"There is bad magic here, I am sure of it."

If you wish to halt, go to 36.

If you wish to continue riding, go to 14.

2

"I do not like either choice!" you cry and rush towards Morgan. But before you can reach her, one of her followers throws a spear at you. It pierces your side and you drop down to the floor, fatally injured. Lancelot gives out a desperate cry as he too is attacked. You lie helpless as your enemies move in for the kill.

You failed at the last hurdle! Go to 1.

3

"We will gladly pay you, gentle knights," you say. You take out a bag of coins and hold them out. The knights move forward, weapons drawn.

The leader laughs. "So willing to pay! What a coward you are!" He turns to the other knights. "Kill them!"

The knights charge towards you, taking you by surprise.

You unsheathe your sword, but are too slow. Your enemies smash at you with their battleaxes and swords, before you crash to the ground.

That wasn't very legendary! Go back to 1 and restart your quest.

4

You unsheathe your sword and leap from your mount, but you are too slow. The demon's jaws snap shut around Lancelot's neck.

In blind fury you charge towards your enemy. The creature gives a shriek of triumph and turns to meet your attack. You swing your sword, but the demon avoids the sharp blade, jumps over your head and leaps onto your back.

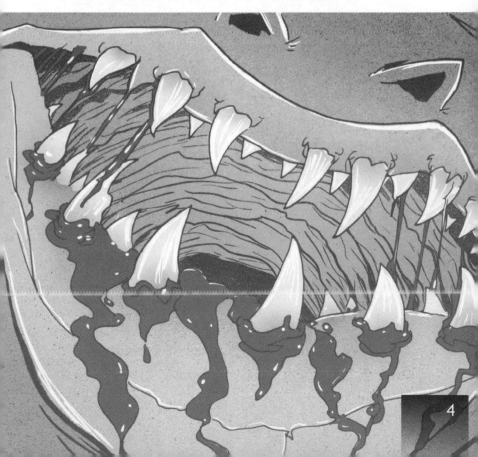

In desperation, you thrash out at the demon, but cannot shake it from your shoulders. You cry out in pain as it plunges its sharp teeth into you. Dropping to the ground, you see the beast open its jaws again, and then there is nothing but blackness...

**You have been defeated by a demon!
Go back to 1.**

5

Before Morgan's followers can react, you leap towards Excalibur, grasp hold of its hilt and try to pull it from the crystal. But despite your efforts, you cannot. It is stuck fast.

Morgan laughs. "My magic is too powerful, Arthur! You must surrender the throne to me..."

Go to 43.

6

"Hold your arm, Lancelot," you order.

There is a flash of light as the hawk suddenly transforms into the figure of a man. You let out a cry of recognition. "Merlin!" You turn to Lancelot. "It is well that you did not shoot!"

The old wizard bows. "My king, I bring grave news. Your sword Excalibur has been stolen from Camelot!"

You shake your head. "How can this be?"

"A monstrous raven flew into the room of the Round Table and took Excalibur from the wall where it hung. The raven flew away before it could be stopped."

"We must head back to Camelot immediately!"
cries Lancelot.

**If you wish to do what Lancelot says, go
to 11.**

**If you wish to hear more from Merlin, go
to 32.**

7

"Who are you?" you ask.

"I am no one of importance," replies the
knight. "But I do know you seek the sword that
was stolen, and I know the secret ways through
the forest. If you spare me I will tell you."

"Very well," you agree.

"You must head to the Crystal Pool and take
the path that passes through the waterfall. This
way will bring you under the earth to the other
side of the forest. The other ways are full of
danger."

Go to 23.

8

You dig your spurs into the horse's flank, but
before it can respond there is a screeching noise

and a rush of air. You are knocked from your saddle as a dark figure smashes into you.

You fall to the ground and look up to see a water demon standing above you, jaws wide open and teeth bared.

Go to 48.

9

"Run!" you cry.

Lancelot obeys and you both hurtle down the tunnel. The dogs give chase as your frightened horses break free, charging past you and pushing you against the rocky walls.

The dogs take their chance and pounce. Lancelot gives a cry as he is overcome by the nightmarish creatures. They tear off his armour and he drops to the ground where he lies motionless. The dogs turn their attention to you.

You stab at the creatures, but there are too many to fight. Seconds later, you too follow your companion into darkness.

Your cowardice has cost you your life! Go back to 1.

"We will ride around the forest," you say, spurring your horse forward.

After several hours of riding, you see six knights mounted on armed chargers, emerge from the trees, blocking your way.

The leader motions you to stop. "Who is it that wishes to pass through our lands?"

"I am Arthur, King of the Britons and this is Lancelot," you reply.

The knights laugh. "Are we supposed to believe that? King or not, no one passes through our lands without paying tribute."

If you wish to pay the knights, go to 3.
If you wish to fight them, go to 30.

11

"You are right, Lancelot," you say. "We need to hurry back to Camelot."

Merlin shakes his head. "My lord, do not be so hasty. There is more that you should know."

You realise Merlin is right.

You must show patience! Go to 32.

12

"Never!" you cry and unsheathe your sword. You rush towards Morgan, and bring your sword down. To your amazement she transforms into a raven and easily avoids your attack. The sword rips into the wooden throne and before you can recover, her followers strike.

You and Lancelot fight bravely, dispatching all those who dare get near you. As you continue your fight, you catch a glimpse of a hawk flying in through a window.

At that moment, Morgan changes back into human form. "Cease your fighting," she orders. Her followers obey. She addresses you. "I say again, surrender Lancelot to me and you may have Excalibur forever."

If you want to surrender Lancelot, go to 29.

If you don't, go to 37.

If you wish to attack Morgan once again, go to 2.

13

"You have tried to kill your king, there can be no mercy," you say.

"Are you sure about this, my lord?" asks Lancelot.

"I am." You carry out your sentence.

"What now?" asks Lancelot.

Go to 40.

14

"We carry on," you tell Lancelot. "It would be foolish to stop."

As you urge your horse forward, you glimpse a dark shape emerging from the river. It is a creature from your worst nightmares! It gives an ear-piercing shriek and speeds towards you with its jaws open, revealing rows of deadly sharp teeth and a long, spiky tongue.

"A water demon!" you cry.

To try and escape the creature's attack, go to 42.

If you want to fight it, go to 28.

15

After several hours of travelling through the tunnels under the Dark Forest, you see daylight ahead. You make your way to the opening, and step out into a valley. The Dark Forest lies behind you. On a hill in front of you stands a large castle.

"That is where we will find Morgan," you say.

If you wish to head to the castle entrance immediately, go to 35.

If you wish to scout out the castle first, go to 25.

"I will fight you myself," you tell the knight.

Ignoring Lancelot's protests, you charge towards the knight, but as you do so, you are blinded by a flash of light and a whirlwind of leaves. Together with Lancelot, you are thrown to the ground.

When the whirlwind subsides, you see there are now two knights sitting on horses in front of you. They are both the same in appearance!

"What trickery is this?" you cry.

Both knights speak at the same time. "All is not what it seems! One of us is real, one is in your imagination. Left is right, and right is wrong! Which of us will you attack? Get it wrong and you will die!"

To attack the knight on the left, go to 38.
To attack the one on the right, go to 49.

17

Before the demon can plunge its teeth into Lancelot's body you spur your horse forward, spear raised. The weapon's sharp point buries itself in the creature's body, and green blood oozes from the wound.

However, the demon is still not defeated — it stands over Lancelot's body, its tongue ready to lash out.

If you wish to continue the fight with your spear, go to 45.

If you wish to use your sword, go to 4.

18

"I am Arthur, King of the Britons!" you cry and spur your horse forward, spear raised. Lancelot follows, but before you can reach the giants, the air is filled with a volley of arrows, shot from the castle walls.

The deadly metal tips pierce your armour and you crash to the ground, mortally injured.

One of the giants moves forward and stands over you with his spiked club raised. "We was expectin' you!" he growls. "My mistress says farewell!"

He brings his club down and all turns to black.

You have failed in your quest. Go to 1.

19

"Lancelot and I will journey through the forest," you say. "Merlin, you must fly to the knights in the north and tell them to hurry to Morgan's castle."

Merlin transforms back into a hawk and flies off, leaving you and Lancelot to begin your journey to the Dark Forest.

After several hours of travelling, you reach

the edge of the vast forest. The way into the forest is dark and narrow. A sense of danger and foreboding passes through your body.

If you wish to head into the forest, go to 34.

If you wish to change your mind and head around the forest, go to 10.

20

You head down the left-hand tunnel.

After sometime you hear a low growling noise. Your horses whinny in fear. Peering into the gloom you can make out the shapes of a pack of monstrous dogs with razor-sharp teeth and burning red eyes.

"Demon dogs," you whisper.

Slowly, the creatures start to make their way towards you. You draw your sword and ready yourself for their attack.

If you wish to fight the creatures, go to 41.
To flee back to the cavern, go to 9.

21

You draw your sword and peer into the white fog.

"Lancelot," you call, but there is no answer.

You move forward and let out a gasp of horror. Lancelot lies against a tree root and standing over him is a creature from your worst nightmares. It turns towards you and howls, revealing its deadly sharp teeth and spiked tongue.

"A water demon!" you mutter.

To use your spear to attack the demon, go to 17.

If you wish to use your sword, go to 4.

If you wish to escape, go to 8.

"I am Arthur, King of the Britons and this is Lancelot," you say. "We wish to speak to Morgan le Fay. Take us to her."

One of the giants smiles, revealing its misshapen, broken teeth. "The mistress was expectin' you. Follow us."

You dismount, and you and Lancelot make your way over the drawbridge. Morgan's followers watch you as you are taken to a great hall, where you see your half-sister sitting on a wooden throne. To her side, Excalibur is set in a block of crystal.

"Welcome, brother," she laughs. "I have your sword and I have made it impossible for you to retrieve it. Are you ready to surrender your crown to me?"

To talk to Morgan, go to 43.
To try and seize Excalibur, go to 5.

23

Before you can say anything, the knight and his horse both vanish into the air, leaving you and Lancelot puzzled at what you have experienced.

You continue on your way, along forest tracks until you come across a sparkling pool of water. At the far end, a waterfall cascades down.

"Which way shall we take?" asks Lancelot.

To continue through the forest, go to 40.

To make your way into the water, go to 33.

24

You remount your horse and continue towards Camelot. After some hours, you see a hawk flying at speed towards you. It hovers briefly above you before swooping down to land ahead of you.

Lancelot nocks an arrow to his bowstring. "Is this another demon?" he asks.

If you wish to shoot the hawk, go to 39.

If you wish to see what happens, go to 6.

25

You and Lancelot move around the edge of the valley to look at the castle more closely. A moat surrounds the castle and there seems to be no way in other than over the closed drawbridge.

If you want to head to the drawbridge, go to 35.

To continue searching for another way into the castle, go to 46.

26

"Lancelot and I will take the safe path around the forest," you say. "Merlin, you must fly to the knights in the north and tell them to hurry to Morgan's castle."

Merlin transforms back into a hawk and flies off, leaving you and Lancelot to begin your journey to the Dark Forest.

After some hours travelling on horseback, you reach the edge of the forest. It stretches for miles.

"Truly, this forest is vast," says Lancelot. "Do we have time to journey around it?"

If you still want to travel around the forest, go to 10.

If you decide to change your mind and head into the forest, go to 34.

27

You choose the right-hand tunnel.

As you head down the passage, you can make out a faint hissing noise, which grows louder and louder. Peering into the gloom, you gasp at the sight before you. The tunnel is full of serpents!

To head back to the cavern and take the left-hand tunnel, go to 20.

If you wish to continue down this tunnel, go to 31.

28

Before you can attack the water demon, it leaps through the air, smashes into Lancelot and sends him crashing to the ground.

The demon stands over him and with a victorious howl, moves in for the kill.

If you wish to use your spear to attack the demon, go to 17.

If you want to use your sword, go to 4.

If you would rather escape, go to 8.

29

You stare at Lancelot. "You are right, my friend. The country is more important than you." Turning to Morgan, you say, "He is yours."

"Take Lancelot away and kill him!" screeches Morgan triumphantly. Your friend is taken from the hall.

"Now you may take Excalibur," says Morgan. "If you can!" she adds.

You take hold of Excalibur but as you do, you feel all the strength vanish from your body. You try to break free, but you can't. You are stuck to the sword and the crystal!

Morgan laughs. "You got what you wished for. You will be with Excalibur forever!"

You chose poorly! To be a legend you must be loyal! Go back to 1.

30

"I am king of these lands," you reply. "It is you who should pay tribute to me!"

"Never," sneers the knight.

"Then you will pay in another way. Lancelot, let us teach these unworthy creatures a lesson."

You and Lancelot unsheathe your swords and do battle. Your fighting skills are too much for the knights, and soon your enemies are defeated. The leader of the knights kneels in front of you.

"Forgive me, my king," he pleads. "Spare my life and I will tell you the secret way through the Dark Forest."

If you wish to spare the knight, go to 47.
If you don't, go to 13.

31

You edge forward, thrashing at the serpents
with your lighted torches. Your horses whinny in
fear as the serpents gather in numbers and spit
poisonous venom at you.

"My lord, we must go back," cries Lancelot,
but it is too late. The creatures coil around your
body and snap at you with their deadly fangs.
You and Lancelot try to fight the serpents, but
there are too many. They slither inside your
armour and bite at you.

Soon you feel the deadly venom course
through your body and you slump down, lifeless.

**You have failed. Start again and go back
to 1.**

32

"Merlin, what more do you know of this?" you
ask.

"I believe that the raven was sent by Morgan
le Fay."

You frown. Morgan is your half-sister and has
studied magic. However, unlike Merlin, she uses
it for evil and not good.

"Excalibur is the symbol of your power,"
continues Merlin, casting an image of the sword.
"With it in her possession, Morgan can gather
together all who are opposed to your rule."

"Then we must win back Excalibur," you say.

"Where has the raven taken it?"

"To Morgan's castle, which lies beyond the Dark Forest," replies Merlin. "The way through the forest is quicker, but full of danger. The way around it is slower but safer."

If you wish to take the dangerous route, go to 19.

If you wish to take the safer one, go to 26.

33

You remember being told about the secret ways through the forest, so you dismount and lead your horse into the water. Lancelot follows you as you head towards the waterfall.

You pass through the crashing water and find yourself in a huge cavern. Using a tinderbox, you and Lancelot light your torches. In the flickering light you make out two large tunnels leading from the cavern.

"Which way now?" asks Lancelot.

To head down the right-hand tunnel, go to 27.

To head down the left-hand tunnel, go to 20.

"The way may be dangerous but we are brave knights," you say and spur your horse into the Dark Forest.

After some time travelling down the narrow track, a knight seated on a charger appears in front of you, blocking your path.

"Who are you, good knight?" you ask.

"I am the Knight With No Name," he replies. "To pass by, one of you must fight me..."

"But I am Arthur, King of the Britons," you say.

"I care not for kings," says the knight.

Lancelot speaks up. "I will fight him, my lord."

If you wish to fight the knight, go to 16.

If you want Lancelot to fight the knight, go to 44.

35

You and Lancelot mount your horses and ride
down the track towards Morgan le Fay's castle.
You soon reach the castle's entrance. The
drawbridge lowers and three giants step out,
armed with wooden spiked clubs.

"Who are you and what do you want?" growls
one of the giants.

If you wish to fight the giants, go to 18.
If you wish to talk to them, go to 22.

36

You bring your horse to a halt.

"We wait here," you tell Lancelot, but there is only silence. You peer into the thickening fog looking for your companion.

"Lancelot!" you cry, but there is still no reply. He has disappeared!

To ride away from this strange place, go to 8.

If you wish to search for Lancelot, go to 21.

37

"I will never betray my friends," you say. "I would rather die."

"I will gladly arrange your request," snarls Morgan.

"I think not," you say. "Friends can be found in places you do not expect them. Merlin, we need your help!"

The hawk darts down and in a flash of light, transforms into Merlin. He touches the crystal enclosing Excalibur and the rock shatters. The sword clatters to the floor and you grab hold of it before anyone can react.

Merlin's voice echoes around the hall.
"The Knights of the Round Table are at the
castle entrance, my liege."

You hold Excalibur aloft. "I am Arthur, and
I am your king. Surrender or suffer the fate
of traitors..."

Morgan's followers hesitate before dropping
to their knees in homage.

"And you, sister," you say.

"I think not," she replies and turns into her raven form. With a screech, she flies out of the window.

"Shall I follow her?" asks Merlin.

You shake your head. "There has been enough death this day, we want no more."

Go to 50.

38

"Left is right and right is wrong," you mutter to yourself. You unsheathe your sword and charge towards the knight on the left.

You swing your sword, tearing open the knight's breastplate. You chose correctly — this is the real knight!

Once more you wield your sword, catching your enemy full on. As the knight falls to the ground, its duplicate vanishes into thin air.

You leap from your horse and stand over your stricken enemy.

If you already know about the Crystal Pool, go to 23.

If you don't know about the pool, go to 7.

39

"Shoot it!" you order. Lancelot lets loose an arrow which hits the hawk.

To your amazement, the bird transforms into the figure of a man. Recognising him, you cry out in distress. "Merlin!"

The wizard lies bleeding on the ground. You rush over, but are too late. The old man is dead, killed by Lancelot's arrow.

Without Merlin's help, you will never defeat your enemies. Go back to 1.

40

"We carry on," you decide.

However, the forest is vast and after several days of travelling, you see a hawk flying towards you. It lands and transforms into Merlin. The old wizard looks grim.

"You are too late, my liege," he says. "Morgan used the power of Excalibur to gather an army and attack the Knights of the Round Table. She has defeated them and now rules Britain."

You have lost the throne! Go back to 1.

41

One of the creatures leaps at you, but you are ready for it. You swing your torch and set light to its fur. The dog yowls in pain and crashes into the other dogs, setting them alight too. The tunnel is filled with demonic sounds and the smell of burning fur.

Using your swords, you and Lancelot make short work of the remaining creatures and continue on your way.

Go to 15.

42

You spur your horse forward but before you can escape, Lancelot cries out in alarm.

You spin your mount around to see your companion lying on the ground. The demon stands over him, jaws open and moving in for the kill.

To use your spear to attack, go to 17.

If you wish to use your sword, go to 4.

If you would rather escape, go to 8.

43

"I will not surrender that which is rightfully mine," you say. "You must return Excalibur to me, now."

Morgan smiles. "Perhaps I will, but I will test what sort of a king you are. I exchange Excalibur for the life of Lancelot. What is more important to you, power or loyalty? Will you give up your friend for your throne?"

Lancelot stares at you. "My lord, the country is more important than my life!"

If you wish to swap Lancelot's life for your throne, go to 29.

If you don't want to, go to 12.

44

"Very well, Lancelot," you say. "Fight for the honour of the Round Table."

But before Lancelot can respond to your command, the knight laughs. "What sort of man are you?" he asks. "Call yourself a king but you're afraid to fight? You are no leader."

Go to 16.

You take hold of your spear and send it hurtling through the air. Your aim is true and it pierces the demon's chest. The creature screams out in agony and falls to the ground.

You leap off your horse to make sure Lancelot is alive. Thankfully he opens his eyes. "Thank you, my lord," he says.

You turn to the demon and hear it mutter. "My mistress will defeat you, Arthur, so-called king..." It breathes its last and the fog instantly disappears.

"What did the creature mean?" asks Lancelot.

You shake your head. "I know not. But we need to be on our guard, of that I am sure."

Go to 24.

46

You make your way around the cliffs overlooking the castle, trying to find a way inside. The way is hard and you search for hours in vain.

Eventually, you see a hawk flying towards you. It lands and transforms into Merlin. "You are too late, my lord. You will not find Morgan here," he says. "She used the power of Excalibur to gather an army and battle against the Knights of the Round Table. She has defeated them, and now rules the land."

You took too long! Go back to 1 and be more decisive!

47

"Tell me," you say.

"You must head through the forest to the Crystal Pool and take the path that passes through the waterfall. This way will bring you safely to the other side of the forest. The other ways are full of danger."

Keeping your word, you allow the knight his freedom.

"Which way shall we take?" asks Lancelot.

If you wish to head into the Dark Forest, go to 34.

If you wish to continue around the forest, go to 40.

48

Desperately, you try to fight off the demon, but it is too powerful. It pins you to the ground and you are overwhelmed by the creature's rancid breath as it lashes you with its spiked tongue.

The creature's teeth briefly hover over your neck, before clamping shut.

Your cry of pain is mercifully short as death takes its grip.

That wasn't very legendary! To restart your adventure, go to 1.

49

You unsheathe your sword and charge towards the knight on the right. You swing your weapon, but the blade merely passes through thin air.

Desperately, you turn your horse around, but as you do, you feel a spear pierce your armour. You crash to the ground, mortally wounded.

The knight stands over you. "You made a bad choice! I told you left was right and right was wrong! You didn't listen. Now you will pay with your life."

These are the last words you hear as he raises his sword and brings it down sharply.

You didn't choose wisely! Go back to 1.

50

You return in triumph to Camelot with the Knights of the Round Table.

Entering the castle you hold up Excalibur to the cheering crowds.

"What will become of Morgan?" asks Lancelot. "Do you think she has gone for good?"

You shake your head. "I am sure we will be hearing from her again. We must be vigilant against her and all those who wish harm to this land."

"With you at its head, we will surely be safe," replies Merlin. "My lord, your name and the exploits of the Knights of the Round Table will be spoken of throughout history. You are truly a legend!"

I HERO

LEGENDS

ATHENA

STEVE BARLOW + STEVE SKIDMORE
ART BY ANDREW TUNNEY

EDGE

You are Athena, goddess of the ancient Greeks and daughter of Zeus, king of the gods. You have left your home on Mount Olympus to help your favourite hero Odysseus escape traps set by Hera, the wife of Zeus. She is powerful, and jealous of your fame. She has the support of Zeus's brother Poseidon, god of the sea, who hates Odysseus.

Even so, despite their plots and schemes, you have brought Odysseus safely back to his home.

You are on Mount Parnassus near the city of Delphi, on your way to visit the Muses, when suddenly you feel sick and dizzy. You are frightened — this has never happened to you before

Your friend the god Apollo appears. "I bring grave news," he tells you. "Hera and Poseidon have convinced Zeus that you have defied him by helping Odysseus. Zeus has banished you from Olympus and taken away your powers...

Continue the adventure in:

IHERO LEGENDS
ATHENA

About the 2Steves

"The 2Steves" are
Britain's most popular
writing double act
for young people,
specialising in comedy
and adventure. They
perform regularly in schools and libraries,
and at festivals, taking the power of words
and story to audiences of all ages.

Together they have written many books,
including the *I HERO Immortals* and *iHorror* series.

About the illustrator:
Andrew Tunney (aka 2hands)

Andrew is a freelance artist and writer based in
Manchester, UK. He has worked in illustration, character
design, comics, print, clothing and live-art. His work
has been featured by Comics Alliance, ArtSlant Street,
DigitMag, The Bluecoat, Starburst and Forbidden Planet.
He earned the nickname "2hands" because he can draw
with both hands at once. He is not ambidextrous; he just
works hard.

Also in the I HERO Legends series:

BEOWULF

978 1 4451 5225 7 pb
978 1 4451 5226 4 ebook

FREYA

978 1 4451 5237 0 pb
978 1 4451 5238 7 ebook

HERCULES

978 1 4451 5228 8 pb
978 1 4451 5229 5 ebook

ROBIN HOOD

978 1 4451 5183 0 pb
978 1 4451 5184 7 ebook

Have you read the I HERO Atlantis Quest mini series?

MENACE FROM THE DEEP

978 1 4451 2867 2 pb
978 1 4451 2868 9 ebook

OCEAN ALLIANCE

978 1 4451 2870 2 pb
978 1 4451 2871 9 ebook

BATTLE FOR THE SEAS

978 1 4451 2876 4 pb
978 1 4451 2877 1 ebook

ATLANTIS ASSAULT

978 1 4451 2873 3 pb
978 1 4451 2874 0 ebook

Also by the 2Steves...

Immortals

HERO

Dragon

Steve Barlow – Steve Skidmore

You are the last Dragon Warrior.
A dark, evil force stirs within the
Iron Mines. Grull the Cruel's
army is on the march! YOU must
stop Grull.

Immortals

HERO

Mermaid

Steve Barlow – Steve Skidmore

You are a noble mermaid –
your father is King Edmar.
The Tritons are attacking your home
of Coral City. YOU must save the Merrow
people by finding the Lady of the Sea.

Immortals

HERO

Superhero

Steve Barlow – Steve Skidmore

You are Olympian, a superhero.
Your enemy, Doctor Robotic,
is turning people into mind slaves.
Now YOU must put a stop to his
plans before it's too late!

Immortals

HERO

Wizard

Steve Barlow – Steve Skidmore

You are a young wizard.
The evil Witch Queen has captured
Prince Bron. Now YOU must rescue
him before she takes control of
Nine Mountain kingdom!